Shine!
Your future is bright...
♡ Naomi Whitnen White

Why Am I Here?

A Child's Book About Purpose

by Naomi V. Dunsen-White

Illustrated by Megan D. Rizzo

Naomi V. Dunsen-White
Why Am I Here?
A Child's Book About Purpose

ISBN: 978-1-955154-08-6

Published by Valley Publishing Co., a division of MAYS Multimedia

www.maysmedia.us Detroit, Michigan, USA
Printed in the United States of America

I dedicate this book to the two people who changed my life forever: my two sons, Keedrick and Austin. Being your mother has given my life purpose. There is no greater joy than knowing that God chose me, just for you. You are my pride and joy!

Your Mom loves you forever.
3 John 4

Why am I here?

Where should I go?

I have a feeling that somebody knows.

Sometimes I sit and
I think about me.

I let my imagination
go wild, go free!

2

When I close my eyes,
what do I see?

Everything is possible.
What will it be?

3

I might see colors,
pretty and bright.

I might see the stars
twinkling at night.

4

I smile when I see
myself tall as a tree.

Strong like a lion
or as small as a bee.

Riding an elephant,
sitting up high.

Or on a giraffe
stretching up
to the sky.

6

Perhaps I will travel.
Where will I go?

Out to the
ocean where
blue waters flow?

Or run through the forest
with tropical friends,

Like colorful birds whose
songs never end.

8

When I grow up,
what will I choose?

I see
amazing things
I could do!

9

I am an astronaut,
exploring the skies.

I am a chef with tasty
dishes to try.

Perhaps I will be a doctor one day.
Or maybe a writer with something to say.

I could be a judge
or a scientist too.

Or create a new
business is what
I will do.

So why am I here?   Where will I go?

I am here to dream,
to learn and grow.

I will go places near, far and wide.

I have a purpose deep down inside.

Although I am probably different from you,

You have a purpose, deep down inside too.

15

One day it will be so easy to see.

Until then... dream and imagine with me!

There may be those
who stand in our way,

To block our success
or ignore what we say.

STOP

NOT YOU

NO

TURN AROUND

17

But nothing can stop
what is now meant to be.

There are blessings in store
for you and for me.

Our skin, our language, we are more than just one.
Our bodies, our culture, where our families come from.

We all have our dreams and a right to belong.
We stand together, united and strong.

You can be anything!
Do you feel it inside?

Do you see
what is possible,
if only you try?

21

Can you imagine what you will achieve?

If you keep reaching high, and if you believe.

22

You are here for a reason.
Yes, that is true.

There is something only
YOU were created to do.

23

Your path to the future was made for YOUR feet.

Special places to go and certain people to meet.

24

All of these things are waiting for you.
Doors that will open for YOU to go through.

So why are YOU here?
Where will YOU go?

Yes, I have a feeling
that somebody knows.

ABOUT THE AUTHOR

Naomi V. Dunsen-White is a children's book author who loves to inspire and encourage children to use their imagination, creativity and interests to discover their potential. She has a passion for closing the diversity gap in the children's literature industry. She believes that when children open their books, they all deserve to see characters who look a lot like themselves.

Naomi has a background in education and social work and loves helping and teaching children. For years, she has enjoyed tutoring children in reading and writing, and believes reading comprehension to be one of the most critical skills for children to master. Naomi believes that encouraging children to become book lovers is one of the greatest opportunities a person could have. She also believes that all children have a gift within, just waiting to be discovered. The joy of reading is the first step toward discovery!

Other Books by the Author

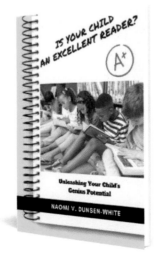

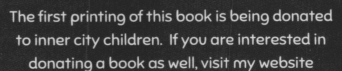

Answer these questions about the story. Answering with a family member or friend is always fun!

1. When you think about what you would like to be when you grow up, what are two of your favorite choices? _____

_____

2. Do you know adults who already made those choices? If you do, write their names here. _____ and _____

3. Ask them to tell you something interesting about what they do. Write it here. _____

_____

4. Of all the colors in the world, which do you like best? _____ 5. Would you describe this color as bright, soft or dark? _____

6. What do you think the word IMAGINE means? _____

_____

7. A story with words that rhyme is often called a _____ 8. What do you like best about this story? _____

_____

9. The girl said "Sometimes I stop and think about me." Can you describe what you think or feel when you think about yourself?

_____

_____

10. Can you explain what the word FUTURE means? _____

_____

11. Take a look at page 17. What do you think the girl and boy should do?

☐ Turn around and go home.   ☐ Look ahead and go toward the future.   ☐ Stay back and wait.

12. Can you explain why you chose that? _____

_____

13. Those first four signs are not positive messages, are they? Can you write positive messages to use instead?

_____   _____   _____   _____

14. What do you think the boy and girl want you to remember most about this story? _____

_____

15. Describe one thing that you would like to see happen in your future. _____

_____

16. Vocabulary and spelling practice. What do these words mean?

judge _____   perhaps _____

ocean _____   astronaut _____

chef _____   purpose _____

ignore _____   culture _____

united _____   special _____